in your hands

in your hands

Carole Boston Weatherford

illustrated by Brian Pinkney

atheneum

Atheneum Books for Young Readers

New York   London   Toronto   Sydney   New Delhi

ATHENEUM BOOKS FOR YOUNG READERS
An imprint of Simon & Schuster Children's Publishing Division
1230 Avenue of the Americas, New York, New York 10020
ATHENEUM BOOKS FOR YOUNG READERS is a registered
trademark of Simon & Schuster, Inc.
Atheneum logo is a trademark of Simon & Schuster, Inc.
For information about special discounts for bulk purchases, please
contact Simon & Schuster Special Sales at 1-866-506-1949 or
business@simonandschuster.com.
The Simon & Schuster Speakers Bureau can bring authors to your
live event. For more information or to book an event, contact
the Simon & Schuster Speakers Bureau at 1-866-248-3049 or visit our
website at www.simonspeakers.com.
Book design by Ann Bobco
The text for this book was set in La Giaconda.
The illustrations for this book were rendered in watercolor, gouache,
and India ink on Strathmore watercolor paper.
Manufactured in China
0617 SCP
First Edition
10 9 8 7 6 5 4 3 2 1
Library of Congress Cataloging-in-Publication Data
Names: Weatherford, Carole Boston, 1956– author. | Pinkney, J. Brian,
illustrator.
Title: In your hands / Carole Boston Weatherford ; illustrated by Brian
Pinkney.
Description: First edition. | New York, NY : Atheneum Books for
Young Readers, [2017] | Summary: "A prayer from mother to son that
he will always be in safe hands"— Provided by publisher.
Identifiers: LCCN 2016016135
ISBN 978-1-4814-6293-8 (hc)
ISBN 978-1-4814-6294-5 (eBook)
Subjects: | CYAC: Mothers and sons—Fiction. | Prayer—Fiction. |
African Americans—Fiction.
Classification: LCC PZ7.W3535 In 2017 | DDC [E]—dc23 LC record
available at https://lccn.loc.gov/2016016135

In memory of the sons we've lost.
In prayer for the sons we love.
—C. B. W.

To the whole wide world.
—B. P.

When you are
newborn,
I hold your hand and study your face.

I name you

Omari—
firstborn son.

I cradle you as you drift to sleep.
While napping, you crack a smile.
I have big, bright dreams for you.

I hold
your
hand

as

you

learn

to walk,

as you cross the street

and enter kindergarten.

I kiss your scrapes and scratches
and wipe your occasional tears.

We take turns
reading bedtime stories aloud.

I tuck you in at night

and remind you of the Golden Rule.

I pour
all the wisdom
that I can
into you.

But I know that I will not always

hold
your hand;

that I cannot always keep you

under
my wing.

Not when you are in the school play
or on the playing field
or at the bus stop.
Not the older you get.

Then, I will hold you in

my
heart

and ask God to hold you in

His
hands.

I will

pray

that you are

safe

in neighborhoods beyond our own
and that you feel confident
when you face new challenges.

I will ask God to guide you
as you test limits
and explore horizons.

I will trust Him
to watch you
as you cross the street

and as you
cross over
to adolescence.

I will pray that
the world sees you as a

child of God;

and, as you cast a longer shadow,
that you will be viewed as a vessel to be steered
rather than a figure to be feared.

I will pray that you are
judged by your character,
and I will call on God
to lead you on the right path.

I will pray
that missteps
bring lessons
and are

forgiven

and that
you be granted

second
chances.

I will pray that you be spared injustice.
And I will ask that if you face old foes,
God bless you with

courage

equal to your

convictions.

I will pray that you can always hold your head up,
and that you grow old

and raise

sons

and

grandsons

who will be exalted
for the suns that they are.

I add my prayers to the chorus:

Black
lives
matter.
Your
life
matters.